Stories
of
Dolls

Susanna Davidson

Illustrated by
Amandine Wanert

Reading Consultant: Alison Kelly
Roehampton University

Contents

Chapter 1

The doll's house

Amy and Tina loved Cherry Tree Cottage. "It's the prettiest doll's house ever," said Tina.

"And Molly's the best doll's owner," Amy added. "We're so lucky to live here."

"You may feel lucky," said Cordelia. "I *don't*!" Cordelia was a beautiful doll and she knew it.

She had golden curls tied up with a shiny clip and a dress that sparkled with sequins.

"I don't belong here," said Cordelia, "I should be in a doll's *palace*. Not stuck in this stuffy, boring cottage."

"It's boring because you never *do* anything," said Amy. "You never help clean or tidy."

"I have more important things to do," snapped Cordelia. "Like brushing my hair."

"Please stop fighting," said Tina. And they had to, as just then they heard Molly.

The dolls rushed back to where Molly had left them and stayed as still as they could.

"It's a sunny day," Molly told them, "so I'm taking you all on a picnic." She carefully picked up the dolls and put them in her basket.

"Oh dear," sighed Cordelia, as Molly set them down on an old rug. "I hope my dress doesn't get dirty."

8

"Look at your sequins and your clip," Tina whispered, to cheer her up. "They're sparkling in the sun."

But far above in the sky, a magpie had spotted Cordelia too. Like all magpies, he loved collecting sparkly things.

The next moment,
he swooped down and
snatched Cordelia up in
his claws.

Let me go!

Cordelia screamed, but the
magpie didn't stop. He flew on
and on, higher and higher.

At last they came to a tall
tree. The magpie dropped
Cordelia into his spiky nest.

"Take me back this second,"
ordered Cordelia.

The magpie shook his
head. "You're mine now,"
he said, then flew away on
his bright, glossy wings.

"Oh!" cried Cordelia. "This is horrible." She spent all day in the nest, feeling lonelier and lonelier.

I'm ruined.

"Please help me," she called to a passing magpie.

"Only if you give me your shiny clip," said the magpie.

12

"I'll give you anything you want," sobbed Cordelia. "Just take me home."

At Cherry Tree Cottage, Molly was putting Amy and Tina to bed. "I'll never see Cordelia again," she thought, sadly.

13

Suddenly, there was a shout. "Molly!" called her mother. "Look who I found by the back door."

There, in the palm of her hand, sat Cordelia. Her curls were ragged and wild and her dress was dirty and torn.

"Cordelia!" cried Molly, carefully tucking her into bed. "I can't believe you're back."

"Nor can I," said Amy, once Molly had left. "I thought you hated Cherry Tree Cottage."

"It's no palace," Cordelia said, "but it's *much* better than a bird's nest. Anyway," she added sadly, "I've lost my sparkle now."

"Never mind," said Amy. "At least you won't be stolen by a magpie again."

Chapter 2

The singing doll

Emily had *always* been Kate's best doll. Kate played with her every day and took her to bed each night.

"And now," Emily told the other toys proudly, "I'm going to the hospital with her."

It's an important job.

"Why is Kate going to the hospital?" asked Teddy.

"She's having her tonsils taken out," said Emily.

"It's not serious," Emily went on. "But she'll need *me* to take care of her."

Next morning, Kate packed her bag. She was going to the hospital that afternoon.

Kate sat nervously on her
bed, hugging Emily. "Don't
worry," Emily told her
silently. "I'll be
with you."

The door opened and Kate's
parents came in. "We've
bought you something," said
her dad, handing her a present.

20

"A new doll!" cried Kate.

"And look," said her mother, "she walks and sings."

Kate ran out of the room, clutching her new doll. "I'm going to show her to all my friends," she said, excitedly.

When Kate came back, she didn't even look at her other toys. She carefully placed the new doll next to her bag and went downstairs.

The other toys crowded around the new doll. "What's your name?" asked Teddy.

"Florinda," she said, with a flick of her long, silky hair.

"Why are you sitting
by Kate's bag?" asked
Emily. She suddenly had
an awful feeling.

"*I'm* going to the hospital
with Kate," said Florinda.
All the toys gasped.

23

"B-b-but," stammered Emily. "You can't go. I'm Kate's best doll. I go everywhere with her."

I always have.

"Not any more," said Florinda, standing up. "Kate doesn't want you now. You can't talk *or* sing."

24

"Yes I can!" Emily insisted.
"But not when she's there.
Look!" said Florinda, pressing
a button on
her tummy.

The next moment a small
CD inside her started to play,
"Mary, Mary, quite contrary,
how does your garden grow?"

"Wow!" said Teddy, impressed.

"Teddy!" said Emily.

"Sorry," said Teddy.

"And that's not all," Florinda added. "If I press this button, I can talk to Emily." And she pressed another button.

"Hello, I'm Florinda," said a tinny voice.

"What else can you do?" asked Teddy.

Florinda pressed a third button. Her legs flew up into the air and she started marching around the room.

"No wonder Kate prefers Florinda," Emily said, glumly. "Ha!" said Florinda. "You don't stand a chance."

"Can you do everything at the same time?" asked Teddy.

"Of course I can!" cried Florinda, pressing every button on her body.

Soon she was marching, talking and singing all at once. "Hello, I'm Mary, Mary, how does your Florinda grow?"

"Stop! Stop!" cried Emily. "I can hear footsteps."

Florinda frantically pressed all her buttons. She stopped talking and walking. But she couldn't stop singing. "How does your garden grow, grow, grow..." sang the tinny voice.

"How strange," said Kate's
mother, coming into the room.
"The doll's turned herself on."
"And she won't stop!" said
Kate's dad, covering his ears.
"Turn her off!"

"I can't," said Kate's mother, pressing the button again and again.

"Grow, grow, grow, grow..." sang Florinda.

"Please fix her," said Kate. "We've got to leave now and I really want to take her."

"Grow, grow, grow, grow..."
sang Florinda.

"There's no time," said
Kate's mother. "You'll just
have to take another toy."

Kate looked around her room. "I'll take Emily," she said, picking her up and hugging her. "She might not be new, but she's still my best doll."

Chapter 3

The lost doll

It was the day of the school fair. Daisy ran from table to table, her rag doll, Ella, bumping behind her.

The toy table was the
best. Daisy propped
up Ella, so she
could see too.

Look!

"There you are!"
said Daisy's mother.
"I've been searching
for you everywhere.
It's time to go home."

She took Daisy's hand and led her to the car. But Daisy had forgotten something...

"I'd like that doll," said a tall man, pointing to Ella.

"No!" thought Ella. "I'm Daisy's." But there was nothing she could do.

Later that evening, the man showed Ella to his daughter. "Look, Sophie!" he said. "I've bought you a new doll."

"But I've got Mia," Sophie replied, holding up her rag doll. Her dad's face fell.

"But thank you," Sophie went on, taking Ella.

That night, as Sophie slept,
Ella lay awake in the dark,
crying silent doll tears.

"What's the matter?" asked
Berry, a large brown bear.

"I miss my owner, Daisy. She
left me at the school fair by
mistake. I don't belong here."

"Don't worry," said Mia.
"We'll help you find Daisy."
"Th-th-thank you,"
sniffed Ella. "But how?"

"I've got an idea," said Berry.
"Sophie must go to the same
school as Daisy. If Ella gets
into Sophie's school bag..."

"...she can go to school and find Daisy," finished Mia. "Brilliant, Berry! Let's put the plan into action tomorrow, when Sophie's at breakfast."

But the next morning, there was a small problem...

SOPHIE

"I'll never reach the bag," sighed Ella. "It's too high." "We'll help!" came a cry from the top shelf. The next moment, a line of tiny monkeys came tumbling down.

"Climb aboard, Ella," cried the nearest monkey.

42

Ella climbed up the monkey chain. Soon, she could almost reach the bag. Then the bedroom door started to open...

"Jump!" cried the monkeys. Ella jumped. Just in time.

43

As Sophie ran to catch the
school bus, she never
guessed who she was
taking with her.

SOPHIE

At school, Sophie dumped her bag in the classroom and rushed off to assembly.

Ella peered out and gasped. The room was huge. "How will I ever find Daisy?" she wondered.

45

And then, at
the other end of
the classroom,
she spotted
Daisy's bag.

When Daisy got home,
she couldn't believe her eyes.
"Look!" she cried, "Ella's come
back to me."

Meanwhile, Sophie couldn't find her new doll anywhere.

"I don't mind," she told her dad, "I only need one doll. But look at the note I found in my bag. I don't understand it..."

Dear Mia, Berry, and the monkeys,

THANK YOU!!
Ella xx

Series editor: Lesley Sims
Designed by Hannah Ahmed

First published in 2006 by Usborne Publishing Ltd., Usborne House,
83-85 Saffron Hill, London EC1N 8RT, England. www.usborne.com
Copyright © 2006 Usborne Publishing Ltd.

48